ALFRED M

by the same author

THE LUNCH-BOX MONSTER

SKIPPER AND SAM

BUT MARTIN! (text by June Counsel)

BEN'S BRAND NEW GLASSES

SAY CHEESE!

Alfred Mouse

written and illustrated by

Carolyn Dinan

faber and faber

LONDON · BOSTON

First published in 1992
by Faber and Faber Limited
3 Queen Square London WC1N 3AU
This paperback edition first published in 1993

Printed in England by Clays Ltd, St Ives plc

A CIP record for this book is available from the British Library

ISBN 0 571 16834 5

2 4 6 8 10 9 7 5 3 1

Contents

For Simon and Richard,
and for Rhianwen and Squeaky.

1 Alfred Mouse

'Goodnight, Ben,' said Mrs Hope. 'Sleep tight in our new house.'

But Ben could not get to sleep. 'Everything's all different,' he complained.

'No, it isn't,' said his mother. 'You've got your old bed and your old curtains and all your old toys around you. You'll soon get used to it here and then you'll love it.'

'I won't,' thought Ben after she had gone. 'It's lonely here. I want to go home.' And then he thought, 'But this is home,' and that didn't cheer him up at all.

Outside Ben's window a tree swayed gently in the breeze. Ben watched the shadows flickering on the brick fireplace opposite his bed. It almost looked as if the fireplace itself was moving . . . Ben blinked, and sat up in bed. It *was* moving. One of the bricks was slowly sliding forward, just as though it was being pushed from behind. He jumped out of bed and ran over to it.

'Mum,' he called. 'Look at this!'

At once the brick stopped moving, but it was sticking out from the rest of the fireplace. When Ben tugged at it it came away easily, leaving a square gap in its place, just big enough for his hand.

The space went back a long way, like a tunnel, but it was too dark to see anything. Ben felt around and suddenly his fingers closed around something warm and furry. He drew his hand out carefully and opened his fingers.

'Oh!' he gasped in astonishment. 'It's a mouse. It's the smallest mouse I've ever seen.'

The little mouse sat on Ben's palm and stared boldly at him with bright, sharp eyes. Its fur was a soft, silky brown, it had tiny, perfect claws on its paws, and a tail that lay in a neat, pink coil over Ben's thumb.

Ben gazed back at the mouse in delight and gently touched the long whiskers around its nose. The mouse squeezed its eyes tight shut, opened its mouth wide, and sneezed very loudly. 'Aachoo,' it went. 'AAAHHHH-

CHOOOO!' And with a scrabble of its scratchy little claws, it leaped out of Ben's hand and vanished into the gap between the bricks.

Ben's mother put her head round the door. 'I thought I heard you calling,' she said. 'Why aren't you in bed?'

'I found a mouse and it sneezed all over me,' said Ben. 'Look, he lives behind that brick in the fireplace. You feel in there.'

'I can't,' said his mother. 'My hand is too big. I don't suppose he wants to be disturbed again. Come on, into bed with you.'

Ben curled up in bed and rubbed his eyes. 'I'll stay awake all night and watch out for that mouse,' he thought. But in no time at all he was fast asleep.

'Ping, ping . . . ping, ping.'

Ben opened his eyes. That sounded like the lift bell on his toy garage. He looked across to where the garage sat on the chest of drawers and, sure enough, the lift was travelling slowly up to the top ramp with a bright red truck on board.

'It's that mouse again,' thought Ben.

'Ping!' The lift reached the top and the truck shot out on to the ramp and careered down the slope to the bottom. It went so fast it sailed right off the edge of the chest and landed upside-down on the floor, CRASH!

Ben picked it up and peered through the windscreen. 'Mouse,' he called gently, 'are you there? Are you all right?'

There was a long silence. Then a small whiskery face appeared from under the driving seat. 'I'm not just "mouse", I'm Alfred Mouse, and I'm not all right at all. That garage of yours is very dangerous. I'm going home.'

'I've got other toys,' said Ben quickly. 'Look, Alfred, this is my best car and it's just the right size for you. It's got a proper motor and a battery inside.'

Alfred ran down Ben's pyjama leg and nipped smartly into the car.

'That's to start the engine,' explained Ben. 'And that lever is to make it go fast . . . Alfred, wait! you need to learn to steer it first.' But, with a screech of tyres and a roar from the engine, Alfred was off.

'Beep, beep,' he shouted, 'out of my way! Zoom, zoommm.'

Ben got his feet into bed just in time as the car raced across the floor and swerved under

the chair. Round and round the room it went, under the bed one end and out the other, and back under the chair again. Ben felt quite dizzy watching and soon his eyes began to close. Zoom, zoom, zoozz, zzzzz . . . Ben was asleep again and, this time, he didn't wake up till morning.

'Did you see that mouse again?' his mother asked him at breakfast.

'Yes,' said Ben. 'He played in my garage and crashed my truck, and then he drove my best car.'

'I think he crashed that too,' said Mrs Hope. 'I heard a terrible noise coming from your room long after dark. Shouldn't he be asleep at that hour?'

'He should,' said Ben. 'But I don't think he

likes to come out in the daytime. Someone might catch him and keep him as a pet. He's not an ordinary mouse.'

'I didn't think he was,' Ben's mother said. 'But you could look after him. It could be your secret.'

Ben loved secrets and so, it turned out, did Alfred.

'You mustn't tell anyone about me,' said Alfred that night. 'Except your mum. I like the sound of her. I might even let her see me.'

'And my Granny,' said Ben. 'You could meet her too if you wanted to. And, maybe, my friend Susie.'

'All right,' agreed Alfred, 'but no one else. You can carry me around in your pocket and no one will know I'm there. You can take me everywhere with you.'

'I don't think Mum would let me do that,' said Ben doubtfully. 'I might lose you.'

'Rubbish!' said Alfred. 'Tell your mother I've never been lost in my life.'

Ben told his mother and she said, 'You tell young Alfred that there's a first time for everything.'

But Alfred never listened when he didn't want to hear.

2 Alfred's Surprising Day

Ben woke up on Saturday morning feeling very pleased.

'I'm going to stay with Granny tonight,' he told Alfred. 'You can come too. We'll have a lovely time.'

'Good,' said Alfred. 'I'd like to meet your Granny.'

After breakfast Mum laid Ben's clothes out on his bed next to his open suitcase. 'I think that's everything you'll need,' she said. 'I'll just ring Granny and tell her when you're arriving and then I'll pack up your things.'

Alfred nipped Ben's ear as Mum went out the door. 'Let's give her a surprise,' he said. 'Let's have the suitcase all packed by the time she gets back.'

'All right,' Ben agreed. 'I can do that. It's easy.'

But it wasn't easy at all. Not with Alfred helping.

'You're too slow, Ben,' he complained, as Ben carefully lifted up his neatly folded shirt and placed it in the case. 'You've got to speed up a bit or your mum will be back before we've finished.' He picked up a pair of shorts in his teeth and hurled them on top of the shirt. 'What about your dirty old dungarees with the special pocket for me? I hope you're bringing those. Look in the wardrobe. And where's your stripy sock for me to sleep in and your plastic turtle for the bath? . . . And you'll want some little cars and a tractor and your woolly blanket and we'd better have a torch . . . put it in, Ben. Now, what else do we need?'

'We're only going for one night,' said Ben.

But Alfred wasn't listening. He jumped up and down on the tumbled heap of clothes and toys that spilled out of the case.

'I'll get this lot nice and flat for you,' he panted. 'You'll never get everything in otherwise . . . Oh! We must ask your mum for some chocolate. We don't want to be hungry. And have you packed your toothbrush?'

'I can't remember.' Ben began to feel horribly muddled.

'Soon find out,' said Alfred. 'I don't know

what you'd do without me, Ben.' He dived into the suitcase and burrowed and kicked his way down to the bottom. There was the sound of rustling and scrabbling and then a squeak of triumph. Alfred re-appeared from under Ben's best jersey.

'Got it! It was in a plastic bag. There was a tube of toothpaste too, but I sat on that rather hard by mistake. I don't think your mum put the top on properly.'

'No,' said Ben, looking at the trail of sticky white blobs that Alfred left behind him, 'I don't think she did.'

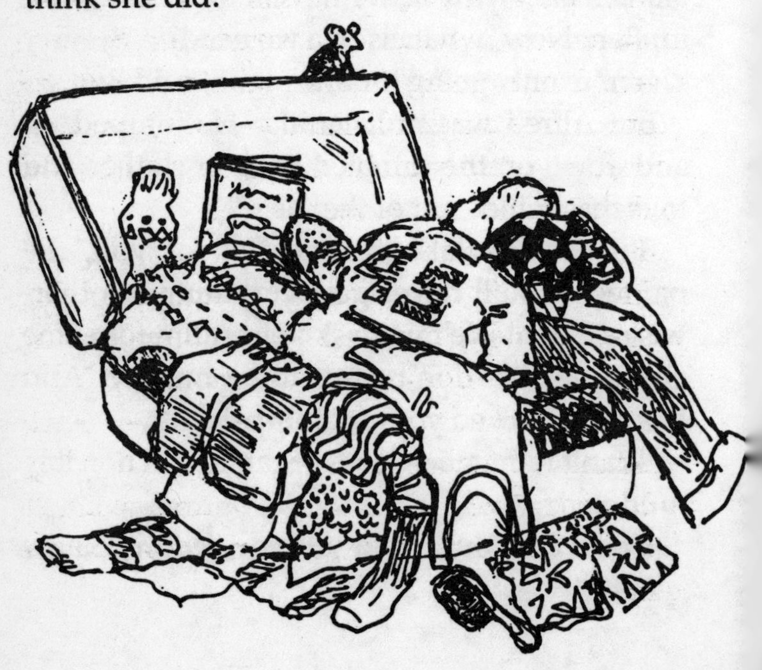

Ben gazed doubtfully at the suitcase. Somehow, it didn't look the same as it did when Mum packed it. It didn't look as though it could possibly shut. And his clothes looked awfully crumpled.

'That suitcase is just too small,' said Alfred, stamping on Ben's jersey and treading the toothpaste blobs well in. 'Put the lid down and sit on it. Anything that falls out, stays out.'

Ben sat on the case. It was very lumpy but he managed to close the lid and even zip it up. There were a lot of clothes still on the bed and on the floor and hanging out of half-opened drawers where Alfred had rummaged through them. Ben decided that he wouldn't wait for Mum to see her surprise. He ran downstairs and out into the garden. 'Come on, Alfred,' he said. 'Race you to the tree!'

But Alfred wasn't there.

'He must still be upstairs,' thought Ben. 'I'll go back and get him.' He ran indoors just in time to see Mum going into his room.

There was a short silence and then 'BEN!' Mum called. 'Come here!'

Ben wandered out into the garden again. It didn't sound as though his surprise had been a great success.

Alfred didn't appear for the rest of the day and he still hadn't turned up when it was time to leave for Granny's house.

'I thought he wanted to come with me,' said Ben, as he set off with Mum for the bus.

'Maybe he gets homesick,' said Mum. 'He's not used to staying in other people's houses. Your suitcase weighs a ton, Ben! What have you got in it?'

'Things I need badly,' said Ben.

Granny was very sorry not to see Alfred. 'I was looking forward to meeting him,' she said. 'You'll have to tell him all about your stay when you get home.'

'I bet he'll wish he'd come with me,' said Ben as he tucked into strawberries and cream. 'I'll save him one strawberry as a treat but he doesn't deserve it.'

'Never mind.' Granny started to clear the table. 'We'll unpack your case, and then you can have a nice hot bath and, after that, I'll read you a story.'

Ben didn't think he wanted Granny to see inside his case. He ran upstairs and into his room. The suitcase was on his bed. Even with the lid closed it still looked very bumpy. One of

the bumps was moving up and down under the lid.

'That's funny,' said Ben to himself. He poked the bump with his finger.

'Oi!' said the bump faintly. 'Get me out of here.'

Ben jumped back in alarm. Then he unzipped the case and peered inside. A very rumpled, very cross Alfred glared back at him.

'I thought you were never going to come,' said Alfred. 'You shut me in here and I've been stuck here all day. I'm hot and I'm squashed and I'm absolutely starving. What's for supper?'

Granny was delighted to see Alfred. She gave him a special supper of sunflower seeds, nuts and raisins, with a big chunk of cheese and the strawberry to finish.

Alfred blew the last crumbs off his whiskers and sat back on Ben's hand with a sigh of satisfaction. 'That's better. What are we going to do now?'

'Ben's going to have a bath,' said Granny. 'I'm going to get his towel from the airing-cupboard right away.'

Alfred waited till she was outside the door, then he leaped on to the floor. 'Quick, Ben! Into the bathroom. Let's give Granny a surprise. We'll have the bath run by the time she gets back.'

They dashed into the bathroom and Ben closed the door.

'Lock it!' squeaked Alfred. 'That'll give us more time.' He jumped into the empty bath, pushed the plug in place, and darted out again. 'Hurry up.'

Ben hesitated. He knew what Mum always said about never locking doors. But the surprise would be even better if Granny had to look for him first. He turned the key in the door. It was difficult as the lock was quite stiff but, finally, he managed it.

'Right!' said Alfred. 'Now for the water.'

Ben turned the cold tap on and the water gushed merrily out. Then he turned the hot tap on as well, very gently, so he didn't get splashed. 'It's easy,' he thought. 'Why won't Mum let me do this at home?'

Alfred tipped bubble-bath into the water as Ben stirred busily.

'That's rather a lot, Alfred.'

'I thought I'd better finish the bottle,' said Alfred. 'Waste not want not. Anyway, it just sort of fell out all at once.'

Ben put his plastic turtle in the bath and went on stirring the water. It began to get too hot so he turned the hot tap off. He needed both hands to do it. The bubbles rose around the turtle and soon covered it altogether. Suddenly he heard Granny calling: 'Ben! Time for your bath.'

Ben and Alfred crouched by the bath and giggled. They heard Granny go into Ben's room and come out again.

'Ben!' she called again. 'Ben? Where have you got to?'

The handle of the bathroom door rattled, but Ben and Alfred didn't move an inch. 'Are you in there, Ben?'

Ben couldn't keep quiet a minute longer. 'Yes,' he shouted. 'And I've got a surprise for you, Granny.'

Granny rattled the door again. 'Open this door at *once*,' she said. She didn't sound as though she was going to like Ben's surprise at all.

Ben heaved a sigh and got up. He grasped the key and tried to turn it in the lock but his hands were wet and slippery from the foamy bath. They just slid round while the key stayed still.

'Stupid key,' he muttered. 'It's all wet now. I can't move it.'

'Well, dry it,' said Alfred impatiently.

Ben rubbed his hands and the key on a towel and tried again. 'It's no good. It won't move.'

'Have a little rest,' said Granny from the other side of the door. 'Then have another go. Don't worry, I'm sure you'll unlock the door next time.'

But he didn't. Ben tried as hard as he could. He gritted his teeth and heaved at the key, but

it was no use. It simply wouldn't budge.

'I think it's stuck,' said Ben in a wobbly voice.

'Are you sure you're turning it the right way?' asked Granny. 'You have to turn it backwards.'

'I know.' Ben tried once more, just in case. 'It won't turn at all and it's hurting my fingers.'

'We'll have to stay here for ever and ever,' said Alfred. 'What are we going to eat?'

'Don't be silly, Alfred,' said Granny rather sharply. 'Now, Ben, wrap a flannel round the key. That will make it easier to hold. There's one on the side of the bath.'

Ben looked round at the bath and his mouth opened in horror. 'Oh, no!' he wailed.

The bubbles had risen high above the bath, almost to the ceiling, and white foam was cascading over the sides and on to the floor. Ben skidded across to the tap to turn it off but the bubbles kept popping in his face and getting in his eyes so he couldn't see properly, and his arms were too short for him to reach easily and get a good grip.

'I can't turn the bath off!' he shouted frantically. 'The tap's too stiff.'

'Don't worry, dear.' Granny sounded a little odd but Ben was past caring about that. 'Just pull the plug out.'

'I can't. I can't find it under all these bubbles . . . Yes, I can! It's stuck!'

'Pull, Ben!' Alfred grappled with the chain while Ben tugged furiously, without success. 'We'd better be quick, the water is nearly at the top of the bath. It's going to overflow any minute. We're going to have a flood in here. HELP!'

Ben had had enough. He sat on the wet floor

and howled as loud as he could.

'Shhh.' Granny rapped on the floor. 'Calm down, you two, and see if Ben can be very clever and take the key out of the door.'

Ben got up and pulled at the key. It came out quite easily. He began to feel better. 'Got it, Granny.'

'Well done. Now, see if you can slide it under the door to me.'

There was a small gap between the bottom of the door and the floor. Ben bent down and gave the key a good shove, but it was just too big to get through.

'Never mind, I'll just have to break the door down,' said Granny. 'Mr Porter next door will help me. We'll have you out in two ticks.'

'Eeoww, bash, crash!' shrieked Alfred happily, as Granny ran downstairs. 'Bazoom, BAM! It'll be like the telly.'

'It won't,' said Ben miserably. 'Wish I'd never listened to you. You and your stupid surprises.'

Alfred turned his back and stuck his nose in the air. Then his round black eyes shone excitedly. He pointed upwards with his paw. 'Look, Ben. The window! Granny could bring a ladder and we could climb out and be rescued.'

'No, we couldn't,' Ben sniffed. 'It's too high, I can't get up to it. And it's too small for Granny to get in.'

'It's not too small for me,' said Alfred. 'Give me that key and put me on the window sill. You can reach if you stand on that stool.'

Alfred nipped out of the window and crept swiftly down through the honeysuckle that grew over the wall below, with the key gripped firmly between his teeth. He landed safely and dropped the key in the middle of the front path. Then he climbed back into the bathroom

as Granny and Mr Porter came through the gate.

'You can tell Granny she won't have to break the door down after all,' he said. 'Won't she be pleased!'

She was very pleased. She unlocked the door and turned off the tap just as the water reached the top of the bath. Then she gave Ben a very soapy, bubbly hug. 'You clever boy,' she said, 'throwing the key out of the window. How did you think of that?'

'He didn't,' said Alfred importantly. 'It was my idea and I did it. I carried the key all the way down to the garden all by myself.'

'Goodness me!' said Granny admiringly. Then she looked steadily at Alfred over the top of her glasses. 'And whose idea was it to lock the door?'

'Er . . .' said Alfred.

'And to run the bath?'

'Ummmm . . .' said Alfred.

'And to tip in all that bubble-bath?'

Alfred closed his eyes and sighed. 'Well,' he said at last, 'Not *all* my ideas are good, Granny.'

Granny started to laugh. 'No,' she said. 'I

think we're going to have to keep an eye on your ideas, Alfred. We don't want you and Ben getting into trouble.'

Later that night, when Ben was tucked up in bed and Alfred was curled up snugly in Ben's stripy sock, Alfred said thoughtfully, 'I think I've gone off surprises. It's all right surprising other people but I always seem to end up getting surprised myself. And that's no fun at all.'

'I know what you mean,' said Ben.

And they went to sleep.

3 Alfred Goes to School

Every night Alfred would say to Ben 'Tell me a story.' And Ben would say, 'A story about what?' And Alfred would say, 'A story about school.' He thought that all Ben's stories were good but best of all he liked hearing about what Ben did at school.

'It does sound fun,' he would sigh wistfully when Ben had finished, 'You're lucky to go to a place like that.'

And then one night he fixed Ben with a beady eye and demanded: 'I want to come too.'

'You can't.' Ben sat up in bed. 'You wouldn't be allowed.'

'Why not? You'd look after me. I could hide in your pocket.'

Ben thought about it. It certainly sounded a reasonable idea but, somehow, Alfred had a way of complicating the simplest plan.

'All right,' Ben agreed reluctantly. 'We've got a Choosing Afternoon tomorrow when we

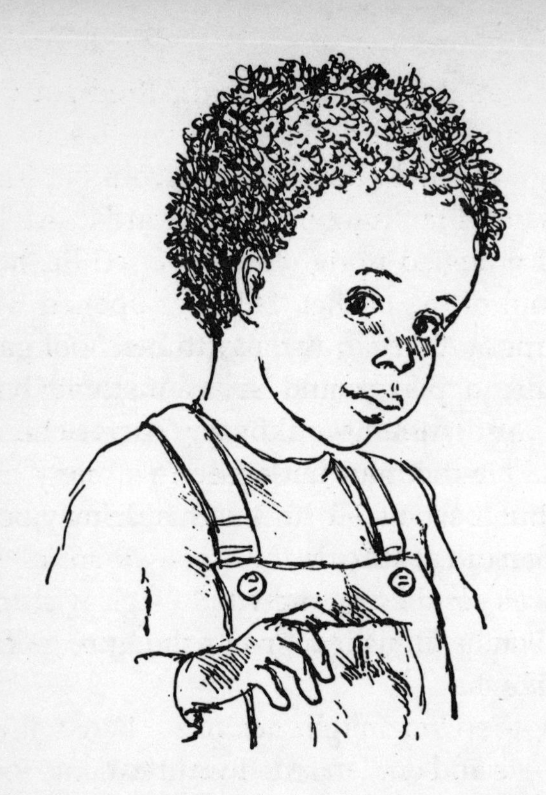

do what we like. You can come to school with me after lunch. But mind you're good.'

'I'm always good,' said Alfred virtuously.

The next afternoon Ben tucked a very excited mouse into the top pocket of his dungarees. 'I'll leave the button undone,' he said, 'so you can see out through the buttonhole, and you can sit on my best blue hanky.'

The school was only round the corner. Ben

skipped all the way there and Alfred got very jogged about. Every time he tried to look out through the hole Ben would give a big jump and send him tumbling backwards. At last Alfred wriggled upright and popped his head right out of the pocket. His eyes opened wide in alarm as Ben ran through the school gates and into a playground swarming with children, all laughing, shouting and chasing around. Alfred had never seen so many children in his whole life and, to his dismay, they all began to head for the open doors of the school as a bell rang loudly.

'I want to go home,' thought Alfred miserably.

He poked Ben in the chest.

'Ow!' said Ben. 'What is it, Alfred?'

'I don't think I'll go to school today,' said Alfred in a casual sort of voice. 'I've changed my mind.'

'Don't be silly. You'll have a lovely time.'

Alfred sneezed loudly and coughed a couple of times. 'I've got a cold,' he croaked hoarsely. 'And I've got a terrible pain.'

Ben looked down at him anxiously. 'Where's your pain?'

'In my tummy . . . all over me . . . oooohh. And my paw hurts. I'm not well enough to go to school today. I'll go tomorrow when I'm better.'

'It's a pity you're ill,' said Ben. 'You'll miss playing in the sand-tray, and you won't hear the story, and there's a little red car that's just the right size for you that you could have driven.'

'I'll see how I go,' said Alfred. 'I may feel just better enough for that sort of thing.'

Inside the school Ben hung his coat on a peg and Alfred looked around. At one table children were busy cutting brightly coloured paper into shapes and at another they were making animals out of big lumps of play dough. Some children were watering the pot plants and others were playing in a neat wooden Wendy house.

'There's no one by the sand-tray,' said Ben. 'Let's start there. You'll like that, Alfred.'

Alfred loved it. He burrowed and tunnelled and rolled in the soft sand and kicked over Ben's carefully turned out shapes. 'I'm staying here all afternoon,' he said.

But at that moment the teacher, Mrs Pearson, clapped her hands; 'You're all a bit dozy this afternoon,' she smiled. 'Shall we have some music to wake us all up?'

Ben dropped his spade. 'Come on. I want to play the trumpet today.'

'I haven't finished my tunnel,' protested Alfred. 'And what about that car ride you promised me?'

'You can do that later,' said Ben and he picked Alfred up, blew the sand off his fur and, ignoring his squeals of protest, dropped him back in his pocket.

After that Alfred was so quiet that Ben began to wonder if he was still there. When Ben felt in his pocket he found it was empty.

Ben looked round desperately. Alfred was so small, he could easily get trodden on or lost. 'I told him to stay with me,' thought Ben crossly. 'Why can't that mouse do as he's told.'

Mrs Pearson took out her guitar and the children clustered round eagerly. They loved hearing her play and would join in enthusiastically with tambourines, wood-blocks and anything else they could find.

'Hurry up, Ben,' she called. 'We're all waiting for you. What are you looking for?'

'Umm . . . the trumpet,' said Ben quickly.

'I've got it,' said Tom firmly, clutching it to his chest. 'And I'm playing it. Let go, Ben. It's mine. *Owww*!'

'*Ben*!' said Mrs Pearson, in her extra-fierce voice, 'Give it back this minute. You can have the xylophone. Now, off we go . . . one . . . two . . . three . . .!'

Ben whacked the xylophone and wished he was hitting Tom instead. Tom grinned and raised the shining yellow trumpet to his lips and blew hard. Nothing happened. He blew again, harder. Still nothing.

'Come on, Tom,' called Mrs Pearson encouragingly. 'We can't hear you over here.'

Tom took a deep breath and blew till his eyes watered and his face was scarlet. Suddenly, with a soft 'Pop,' a bundled-up blue handkerchief shot out of the trumpet and sailed across the room. 'PARP!' went the trumpet as the handkerchief landed on Ben's xylophone. 'Parp-PARP-PAAARRRRPPPP!' And 'Ting-tong-tang,' went Alfred on the xylophone and he jumped out of the handkerchief and scuttled along the keys. 'Tan-tong-ting-ting-tong-tang-tung-toonggg.'

'Got you!' said Ben. 'Now stay in my pocket.'

'Ben stuck his hanky up Tom's trumpet,' said Kim. 'Wasn't that a bad thing to do, Mrs Pearson?'

'Very bad,' said Mrs Pearson. 'But he's done some lovely playing on the xylophone so I think we'll forgive him this time.'

Ben went red. He could see his top pocket shaking with Alfred's laughter. 'You behave,' he whispered furiously. 'Or I'll never take you to school with me again.'

'I'm sorry,' said Alfred in a small voice. 'I didn't mean it. It was just a joke. Let's do a painting next. That'll cheer us up.'

'All right.' Ben chose an easel in the corner and put on an overall.

'It's gone all dark in here,' complained Alfred. 'I can't see.'

Ben sighed, fished him out from under the overall, and sat him behind a paintpot on the ledge of the easel. 'You can watch me paint,' he said.

'I want to paint a picture too,' said Alfred.

'Shhh. You can't.' Ben dipped the brush in the yellow paint and made a round smiling sun.

'Cheese.' Alfred gazed at it longingly. 'Yum yum. I want to paint *now*. I'm going to paint a chocolate biscuit.'

'No,' said Ben. 'Anyway, the brushes are much too big and heavy for you. You couldn't hold them.' He picked the brush out of the green pot and painted a sweeping, grassy hill.

Alfred twitched his tail sulkily. 'Boring, boring, boring,' he muttered. 'Wish I hadn't come.'

Ben ignored him and painted a blue car on the hill. He was so involved in his picture that he didn't notice when Alfred suddenly stopped sulking and nipped round to the other side of the double easel. A clean sheet of paper was clipped to the board and on the ledge below were six full pots of paint with a brush in each.

'Ah ha!' said Alfred, rubbing his paws. 'That's more like it. Though who needs a brush with a magnificent tail like mine?'

Ben had just finished his picture when Alfred returned. He stared at the mouse in horror. 'What have you done to yourself? You're all covered in paint.'

Alfred looked down at himself. 'I've been painting the biggest strawberry you ever saw, and I didn't want the colours to get mixed up,' he explained. 'So I used my tail for the red paint and my front paws for the blue in the sky, and I was trying to paint the green leaves with my back paws when I fell in the paintpot. It's a good job I can swim,' he added severely. 'I thought you were meant to be looking after me.'

For once Ben heaved a sigh of relief when the day ended.

'How did Alfred get on?' asked Mum, on the way home. 'I can guess he's been painting.'

'He was very naughty,' said Ben.

'I was good,' said Alfred smugly. 'I worked so hard that I shall have to have a sleep when I get home. I don't want to be tired at school tomorrow.'

After the children had gone home Mrs Pearson and her helper, Jackie, started to clear up.

'Look at this,' said Mrs Pearson. 'I think it's the smallest painting I've ever seen.'

'And it's surrounded by the biggest mess!' said Jackie. 'I've spent ages trying to mop all the paint off the floor but it's still everywhere.'

'I wonder what it's meant to be?' Mrs Pearson examined the picture closely. 'It looks like a ladybird or, possibly a redcurrant. We'll put it up on the wall tomorrow and ask the children who painted it.'

'Perhaps a mouse did it,' Jackie said jokingly. 'Have you seen these specks of paint?' They look exactly like tiny paw prints all over the floor.'

Mrs Pearson laughed. 'A mouse at school! That'll be the day. Really, Jackie, what will you think of next!'

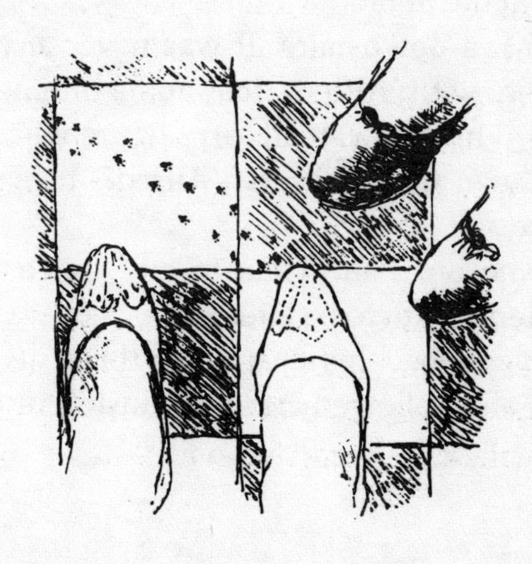

4 Alfred and the Wrong Pocket

'I'm going to the clinic today,' said Ben. 'I'm going to have a special injection.'

'I'm coming to the clinic too,' said Alfred.

Ben laughed. 'Don't be silly. Mice don't go to the clinic.'

'Why not?' said Alfred. 'I want an injection too. It's not fair. You never let me do anything.'

'I've got to go now,' said Ben quickly. 'That's Susie at the door.'

Ben ran downstairs. It was never any good arguing with Alfred. Just for a moment he thought he saw a small furry figure whizz past him down the banisters. 'Alfred?' he said. 'Is that you?'

'Come on, Ben. Time to go,' called Mum. 'We don't want to be late.'

Ben grabbed his coat from the foot of the stairs and followed her and Susie out of the door.

It was warm and stuffy in the clinic. Ben and Susie sat on the hard chairs and wriggled with boredom.

'I'm boiled,' complained Ben.

'Me too,' said Susie.

'Well, take your duffle coats off,' said Mum. 'Give them to me and I'll look after them. Why don't you have a ride on the rocking-horse? You always used to love that when you were little.'

So Ben and Susie each had a turn on the rocking-horse but, somehow, it seemed smaller than they remembered, and not as much fun.

'You've just got bigger.' Mum smiled.

At last the nurse put her head round the door: 'Ben and Susie, would you come through now, please. My, haven't you two grown!'

'All that waiting and all that fuss,' said Ben in astonishment afterwards. 'And the injection only took a minute.'

'It only took two seconds,' said Susie, who did like to get things right.

Mum and Ben dropped Susie off at her house and walked on home. Ben felt hot and

uncomfortable. His coat felt too tight under his arms and it would hardly fasten across his chest. 'Of course!' he thought to himself. 'I've grown. Everyone said I had at the clinic, but I never knew it could happen so fast. I'm sure I was my usual size this morning.' He put his hands in his pockets but even they didn't feel right because both his pockets were empty.

'Where's my monster conker gone? And my giant petrol marble and my fossil stone and that toffee I never finished . . . And where are those football stickers I was going to swap with Tom?' He felt right into the corner of the lining and suddenly his fingers caught on some frayed threads and went straight through into empty space.

'Mum!' Ben cried in alarm. 'I've got a ginormous hole in my pocket and all my best treasures have fallen out.'

'Oh, Ben. Why didn't you tell me before? I would have mended it.'

'It wasn't there before,' said Ben.

'Ginormous holes don't appear overnight,' said Mum.

'This one did,' said Ben.

At that moment there was a crack of thunder and a sudden downpour.

'Run!' exclaimed Mum. 'I'm sorry, Ben, we'll have to look for your things tomorrow. It's much too wet to stay out now.'

That night, when Ben went to bed, he couldn't understand why Alfred didn't appear. He took the brick out of the fireplace and put his hand right inside and felt about, but Alfred wasn't there.

'I expect he's having a sleep somewhere,' said Mum. 'He'll turn up in the morning.'

But Alfred didn't turn up in the morning, nor in the afternoon. Ben looked everywhere. He opened all his drawers and cupboards in case Alfred was trapped inside. He shook out all his shoes and turned all his cars and space ships upside down. But Alfred was nowhere to be found.

'He's never gone off for so long before,' said Ben. 'Something awful must have happened to him.'

'Are you sure you didn't take him out anywhere?' asked Mum.

'Quite sure,' said Ben miserably. Then he stopped and thought and, suddenly, he wasn't sure at all. Alfred had wanted to go to the clinic and Alfred usually did what he wanted to do. Ben remembered the small figure flying down the banisters. 'My coat was hanging on the stairs. He could have hidden in the pocket.'

A very nasty thought began to creep into Ben's mind. It was such a nasty thought that he wouldn't let it in at first but, in the end, he had to. Alfred must have hidden in his pocket on the way to the clinic but Alfred certainly hadn't been there on the way back. He must have fallen out through the hole on to the street. No wonder he wasn't behind the brick in the fireplace. He was alone and lost, far away in the town, and he would never be able to find his way home.

'Don't worry,' said Mum, who must have had the same thought, 'we'll walk back to the clinic and we'll search every inch of the way for Alfred. We'll soon find him.'

'We won't,' wailed Ben. 'He's so little. We could miss him easily.'

'Well, we're big enough,' said Mum. 'And Alfred has very sharp eyes. He'll just have to find us.'

But, though they walked to and fro all the way to the clinic, and even looked all round the clinic itself, there was no sign of Alfred.

They were about to give up and go home when they saw Aunty Jo and Susie coming towards them.

'Come and play at my house,' called Susie.

'No,' said Ben.

'We've made some gingerbread,' said Aunty Jo. 'Do come, Ben. I'm sure your mum would like a cup of tea too.'

Ben trailed along gloomily. He didn't want to play with Susie. He wanted to play with Alfred. And he wasn't going to eat till he found him.

Aunty Jo opened her front door. 'I'll put the kettle on right away,' she said. 'Susie, get the cake out, and mind that cat.'

A big black cat stalked up to greet them. He jumped up at Susie and started to paw at her coat, purring loudly.

'Down, Pitch,' scolded Aunty Jo. 'That cat! I don't know what's got into him since yesterday. He won't leave Susie alone and he's been miaowing all over the place.' She clapped her hands and shooed Pitch into the garden.

Ben and Susie threw their coats on the stairs and ran up to Susie's room. Ben told Susie all about the missing Alfred. Susie let Ben have first go on her new train set and Ben watched the train go round and round the track and tried not to think about how much Alfred would have enjoyed driving the engine.

'Don't worry, Ben,' said Susie. 'Alfred will find his way home. I know he will.'

Ben almost believed her. He had two slices of gingerbread and a long drink of fruit juice and, by the time Mum was ready to go home, he was feeling more cheerful.

Aunty Jo picked up the coats from the stairs. 'Look at these,' she sighed. 'When will you learn to hang things up? Now, which coat is which? They both look the same to me.'

'My one is a bit bigger than Susie's,' said Ben.

'My one has a great big hole in the pocket,' said Susie.

'WHAT?' said Mum. She took one of the coats and felt in the pockets. Then she handed it to Ben with a smile. 'This one is yours,' she said.

Ben put on his coat. It felt just right and not too tight any more. 'I must have shrunk,' Ben decided. 'It's all that eating I haven't been doing.' He put his hands in his pockets and his fingers closed round something hard and round and smooth. 'My giant petrol marble! It's back. And my monster conker and my fossil stone and my football sticker and . . . and . . .'

'Where on *earth* have you been?' demanded Alfred.

That night, Alfred sat on Ben's bed and washed himself from head to tail. 'I've got that revolting sticky toffee of yours all over my fur,' he complained. 'But I got so hungry I had to eat it.'

'I thought I'd lost you,' said Ben.

'I thought I'd lost me too,' said Alfred. 'I couldn't think where I'd got to, and I didn't dare look in case that horrible cat caught me and gobbled me up. Honestly, Ben, I don't know how you could have got the coats muddled. One sniff would have told me I had got the wrong one.'

'It wasn't my fault. You shouldn't have come.'

'I know,' said Alfred sadly. 'I won't do that again . . . but did you bring me an injection?'

'Of course not.' Ben rolled up his sleeve and showed Alfred the faint mark on his arm. 'It's a sort of needle prick. I couldn't bring you that.'

'A needle prick!' gasped Alfred in disgust. 'I thought it was something nice to eat.'

'Well, I did get a lump of sugar too,' said Ben. 'And I brought one for you, just for once.'

'That's different,' said Alfred happily. 'Why didn't you tell me that before?' And he hopped behind the fireplace with the sugar lump, and was scrunching away noisily as Ben fell asleep.

5 Alfred Goes to Tea with Granny

Ben was digging a hole. He had been digging it for days and days but he didn't mind. Sometimes it was a hole for laying telephone wires and sometimes it was a trap for wild beasts and sometimes it was just a hole. Today it was a secret tunnel to his grandmother's house. Alfred sat on his shoulder and watched critically.

'Why don't you use your spade?' he asked.

'It's broken. I hit it on a stone yesterday and the head fell off, so I'm using the handle and my fingers now.'

Alfred ran down Ben's arm and along the spade handle into the hole. 'You're doing it all wrong,' he said. 'Watch me. I'll soon show you how to do it.' And he burrowed his nose into the damp earth and started to kick backwards frantically with all his paws at once. Lumps of earth and pebbles flew in all directions and soon Alfred's coat was thick with grey mud.

At last he sat back, blew some bits of dead leaf off his whiskers and waved a paw at Ben. 'How about that?' he said proudly.

Ben didn't think that the hole looked any deeper; if anything Alfred seemed to have kicked rather a lot of earth back into it, but he didn't like to say so. 'I think Mum's calling,' he said.

Ben's mother had been calling for quite some time, but he had been too busy to take any notice before.

'There you are!' she said. 'Oh, Ben, what have you been doing? I thought you were all ready to go.'

'Go?' asked Alfred. 'Go where?'

'We're going to Granny's,' said Ben. 'She's going to look after us while Mum goes shopping. I bet she's made a special tea for us.'

'Good,' said Alfred. 'I like your granny and I do like her special teas. But I'm not going anywhere near her bathroom.'

'You're awfully dirty, Alfred.' Ben looked at him doubtfully.

'I'm quite clean enough,' replied Alfred cheekily. 'Granny won't mind. She'll like me just as I am. I think I'll hide in your pocket before your mother sees me though. She's funny about mud.'

Alfred was right about Ben's mother. She didn't like mud at all and she wasn't a bit pleased with Ben. 'Look at your hands!' she scolded. 'You can't go out to tea with such dirty nails. What will Granny say when she sees you?'

Ben thought about it. 'She'll say, "Hello Ben! How lovely to see you. How about a big kiss?"'

Mrs Hope shook her head crossly. 'We haven't got time to argue. Hurry up or we'll miss the bus.'

Granny was looking out of the window

when they arrived and she opened the door at once as Ben ran up the path.

'Hello, Ben!' she called. 'How lovely to see you. How about a big kiss?'

Ben gave her one. Then he hugged his mother and they waved goodbye to her as she set out for the shops. Finally Ben took Alfred out of his pocket and held him up to his grandmother.

'I've brought Alfred too,' he said. 'Here he is.'

Granny looked very puzzled. 'Oh, no,' she said, after a long pause. 'Oh dear, no. That's not Alfred. What a shame. I was so looking forward to seeing him again. I'd

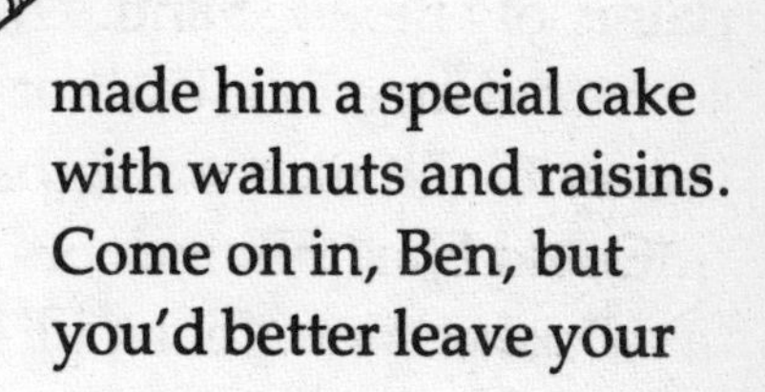

made him a special cake with walnuts and raisins. Come on in, Ben, but you'd better leave your new friend outside. He looks like a garden mouse to me.'

'I'm *not* a garden mouse, I'm ALFRED!' roared Alfred, as loud as he could. 'Tell your granny to put her glasses on, Ben.'

'Now, there's no need to be rude,' said Granny. 'I can see perfectly well and he is certainly not my friend Alfred. For a start, this is a grey mouse and Alfred is chestnut brown. This mouse has stiff, spiky fur but Alfred's fur is smooth and soft. And Alfred's paws are pink, and he has very white teeth.'

Alfred examined his paws quietly. They were definitely not pink any more, so he hid them behind his back. Then he gave Granny his best grin.

Granny peered a little closer. 'Well now, I must say, your teeth do look very like Alfred's . . . but, no, you can't be Alfred. Leave him in the garden, Ben.'

Alfred hopped up and down in a fury on the palm of Ben's hand. 'Do something,' he squeaked angrily. 'Walnut and raisin cake! My favourite. Think of something quickly!'

'Could I just run indoors and wash my hands first?' asked Ben. 'Then I'll leave him outside.'

'Good boy. I'll be getting your tea ready.' Granny went into the kitchen.

Ben popped Alfred back in his pocket and ran upstairs. Alfred would have to go in the bathroom after all. Ben put the plug in the basin and turned the taps on full. Then he rolled up his sleeves and picked up a bar of soap.

'Out you come, Alfred. Bath's ready.'

Alfred ran up Ben's jersey and stood balanced on the edge of the basin.

'Call that a bath?' he demanded in disgust. 'I always have my bath in a nice tub of dry saw-dust. I'll get soaked in there.'

'That's the idea,' said Ben. 'Jump in.'

'No,' said Alfred firmly. 'It's much too wet. It's bad for me to get wet. I could get a chill.'

'Oh, dear.' Ben rinsed the soap off his hands. 'You'd better keep away from the basin then. You don't want to fall in . . . watch out!'

But it was too late. Alfred had overbalanced, SPLASH. Down, down he went into the warm water, and up he came again, spluttering and coughing. 'Ooohh,' he moaned. 'Oooohh, it's horrible. Get me out of here.'

'I will,' said Ben. 'If you'll just keep still for one minute.'

But Alfred couldn't keep still. He swam up and down frantically and the water grew steadily muddier. Suddenly he began to enjoy himself.

'I don't think much of this water, though,' he complained. 'It's not clean and clear like the water you have at home.'

So Ben changed the water and stirred it into

waves while Alfred swam six lengths of the basin.

'Time to get out,' said Ben.

'I'm not ready yet.' Alfred swam another length. 'Put some more water in.'

'Come on, Alfred. Out!'

'No.' Alfred turned over and floated on his back. 'I'm staying in.'

'Tea's ready,' called Granny from downstairs.

'Hurry up, get me out,' shouted Alfred. 'This basin's all slippery and slidey.'

Ben scooped him out and stood well back as the little mouse shook himself vigorously, sending a spray of water all over the bathroom.

Then he let Ben wrap him in a clean face flannel and rub his fur dry. He closed his eyes and hummed contentedly.

'Now,' said Ben, 'look in the mirror.'

'I look just like me,' said Alfred. 'Granny will recognize me now. She *will* be pleased to see me.'

Granny was waiting downstairs with the tea laid out on a table. 'Come and sit down, Ben.' She smiled. 'I hope you're hungry.'

Ben held out his hands, palm upwards, and

Alfred ran out of his sleeve.

'What lovely clean hands . . .' began Granny approvingly. 'Oh! There you are, Alfred. You did come after all. I was afraid Ben had left you behind. He brought a very peculiar mouse with him who pretended to be you, but he couldn't fool me.'

Alfred opened his mouth and shut it again as Ben winked at him and handed him a very large slice of walnut and raisin cake.

6 Alfred Goes Shopping

'I don't know why it is,' said Ben to Susie, as Mum led them into the big department store in town, 'but whenever we go shopping for shoes Mum ends up cross.'

'My mum's the same,' said Susie. 'She likes such awful ones. I always say they hurt, and then she can't buy them.'

They stepped on to the moving staircase.

'Pity you couldn't bring Alfred. Wouldn't he love running up and down this!'

A small head appeared from Ben's sleeve. 'What's that? What would I love doing?'

Ben pushed him back again. 'Nothing. Don't let Mum see you.'

The shoe department was very busy and lots of people were waiting impatiently to be served. There was a machine at the entrance with a pink ticket sticking out of it.

'That's our number in the queue,' said Mum, pulling out the ticket. 'When they call out

"twenty one" it's our turn.'

'I'll look after it,' said Ben.

'No, me,' said Susie. But Ben grabbed it. Susie tried to open his fingers and twist it out of his hand but Ben clenched his fist and shoved it deep in his pocket.

'Stop fighting, you two, and sit down,' said Mum. 'I'll get you some shoes to look at while we're waiting. How about these, Susie? They look just right for school.'

'No,' said Susie. 'Alfred doesn't like brown shoes.'

'Alfred isn't going to wear them,' said Mum.

'Nineteen,' called one of the assistants.

'Soon be our turn,' said Mum. 'Now, put those down Susie. You don't want those.'

'Yes, I do!' Susie kicked off her old shoes. 'They're lovely and shiny and they've got real high heels.'

'I like the spotty bows on the toes,' said Ben. 'Walk up and down in them, Susie.'

'They're too big,' said Mum firmly. 'You'll fall over in those. Let's see what else we can find.'

'Twenty,' called another assistant.

'We're next,' said Mum. 'Give me back the ticket, please, Ben.'

'Twenty-one!'

'That's us.' Mum waved at the assistant. 'Hurry up, Ben.'

Ben felt in his pocket and pulled out some tattered scraps of pink paper. 'I'm afraid Alfred's eaten most of it.'

'Alfred?' Mum exclaimed crossly. 'I thought we'd agreed we were leaving Alfred at home today.'

'I know.' Ben sighed. 'I did tell him.'

'He's a very disobedient mouse,' said Susie primly.

The sales assistant peered doubtfully at the bits. 'I can't see the number of those. You'll have to get another ticket.'

'Right,' said Mum grimly when they all sat down again. 'This time I look after the ticket. And take those boots off, Susie. You can't wear red suede ankle boots to school.'

Susie stuck out her lower lip and scowled. 'Alfred says these are the best. He's looked all round inside them and he says they're all nice and soft and pretty.'

'Are you two telling me,' asked Mum in a low and very fierce voice, 'that you've let that mouse loose in this shop? Because if so, you'd better get him back at once. We're not spending the whole afternoon looking for him.'

Ben nudged Susie. 'I told you so,' he whispered. 'She's getting cross already. Come back, Alfred.'

'I was only trying to help,' said Alfred, climbing back up Ben's leg. 'I've seen some lovely black shoes over there with stripy laces and squidgy soles. Why don't you try them on?'

'All right,' said Ben. 'Later.'

At last it was their turn. The assistant was young and cheerful. He measured their feet carefully and came back with an armful of boxes. 'We'll soon have you fixed up,' he said confidently.

There were shoes in every shade of brown. Shoes with straps, with buttons, with laces and with Velcro fastenings. Plain shoes and shoes with fringes and shoes with patterns punched on the toes. Alfred darted in and out of the open boxes, examining each shoe closely.

'They are no good,' he told Ben. 'They've got nasty rough seams inside.' And, 'Don't have those, Susie, the buckles are too stiff.'

'They can't all be so uncomfortable,' said Mum suspiciously as Ben and Susie limped up and down the room and the assistant opened box after box.

'These ones are pinching my toes,' Susie complained.

'And these ones are rubbing my heel,' said Ben. 'Alfred says I'll get blisters.'

'Tell that mouse to mind his own business,' said Mum. 'What does he know about shoes? Now, let's see what else we can find.'

'I'm afraid that's the lot,' said the assistant. 'That's all the brown shoes we've got.'

They all sat and looked at the pile of boxes and discarded shoes in silence. Even the cheerful assistant didn't look cheerful any more.

'Oh, dear,' said Mum at last. 'I think we'll have to call it a day.'

Suddenly Ben jumped up and ran to the display shelf. He took down a shoe. 'This is the one that Alfred likes. He says it would be just right for school and Susie could have the same.'

'I don't care *what* Alfred says . . .' Then Mum stopped. She looked at the shoe. 'Right. Let's see if they come in your sizes.'

Five minutes later Ben and Susie wriggled

their toes in their smart new black shoes with the black and yellow striped laces and the squidgy soles.

'Very nice,' said Alfred, peering down from Ben's pocket. 'I told you I'd find you some good shoes and I did, didn't I?'

7 Alfred and the Babysitter

Ben was in bed with a cold and a headache and Alfred was doing acrobatics. Alfred ran up the back of Ben's basketwork chair and hung upside down from the top. Then he caught the blind cord between his paws, took a running jump, and swung as high as he could go.

'Watch me, Ben. Wheeeeee!'

Ben laughed: 'I do that at the playground.'

Alfred stopped swinging. 'I know,' he said, 'and you never take me. You do all my favourite things and you leave me behind. I want to go to the playground too.'

'You can't. It's too dangerous. Someone might tread on you or you might fall off something. You're too little.'

'I could stay in your top pocket like I did at school. You could button it up so I don't fall out.'

'You won't be able to breathe if I button you in,' said Ben.

'Yes, I will,' said Alfred, 'I've bitten a little hole in the front specially.'

Ben's mother came in and sat on the bed.

'I have to go to work now, Ben,' she said. 'But you've got a babysitter to look after you this morning. Mrs Dunstan . . .'

'Oh, no!' wailed Ben. 'I don't like that Mrs Dustbin. Alfred can look after me.'

'I think he's a bit small to do that. Now, don't make a fuss, Ben. I think you're going to have a lovely time with your babysitter.

'No, I won't,' said Ben, as Mum went downstairs.

'What's wrong with Mrs Dustbin?' asked Alfred. 'I like the sound of her. She's got a beautiful name.'

'She's horrible,' said Ben. 'She's got great big teeth and she's all whiskery.'

'Whiskers are nice,' said Alfred reproachfully, 'and very useful. I wouldn't be without my whiskers for anything.'

'Huh.' Ben wasn't impressed. 'I'm going to sleep and I'm not waking up till Mum comes home.'

*

Some time later Ben heard footsteps outside his open door.

'Are you all right, Ben?'

'Mmmm.' Ben kept his eyes tight shut till the footsteps went away. Then he sat up in bed.

He felt much better and his head didn't hurt any more. Alfred was crouching on the window sill with his nose pressed against the glass and his tail switching to and fro with excitement.

'Take a look out there,' he squeaked.

Ben looked out of the window. The sun shone down on the quiet, empty road. Even the playground on the corner was still and peaceful. Usually it was crowded with shouting, laughing children, and Ben had to queue up for ages for his turn. But now it was almost deserted. A couple of toddlers were being pushed up and down on the see-saw by their parents but the slide, swings and climbing frame all stood invitingly, waiting for someone to play on them.

Alfred turned and stared hopefully at Ben. 'Let's go to the playground *now*!' he said. 'Everyone is at school. I wouldn't get knocked about or trodden on or anything.'

'We can't do that,' said Ben. 'I'm not allowed to go alone. It's too dangerous. We might fall off something and there wouldn't be anyone to pick us up.'

'Those people by the see-saw could look after us. Just think, we could go on everything as often as we liked.'

Ben hesitated. 'What about old Mrs Dustbin?'

'She thinks you're fast asleep. We'll be back

before she notices we've gone.'

Ben jumped out of bed and threw on his clothes. He tucked Alfred into his top pocket. 'All right, Alfred. We'll go for five minutes. But you've got to be as quiet as . . .'

'As a mouse,' finished Alfred smugly.

Ben tiptoed downstairs. He slipped into the garden and was just about to climb over the fence when he saw his big cousin, James, watering Mum's tomatoes.

'Hi!' said James. 'Feeling better? I've got the day off school, so I said I'd help your mum out. Want to do some gardening?'

Ben liked James. He had a round, merry face and spiky hair. He wore baseball caps and baggy track suits and big trainers with thick soles. When he grinned he showed two rows of shiny metal braces on his teeth. Ben longed to be exactly like him.

Alfred glared impatiently through the hole in Ben's pocket.

'What's the delay?' he demanded. 'I want to go to the playground *now*!'

'We can go to the playground if you like,' said James to Ben. 'We'll go out through the side gate.'

Ben opened his mouth and shut it. He couldn't tell James he had a babysitter, not when James was treating him like a proper friend. It sounded much too babyish.

He watched nervously as James locked the back door. What if Mrs Dustbin wanted to get into the garden? What if she went upstairs and found his empty bed?'

'Better keep warm,' said James, and he put his baseball cap on Ben's head and zipped Ben's jacket up to the neck. 'How's that?'

'Oi!' came Alfred's muffled voice from underneath. 'What's going on? Are we at the playground yet?'

Ben didn't hear because the cap covered his ears, and it rested on his nose so he had to tilt his head back to see anything, but he didn't mind. It was just the sort of cap he had always wanted. He forgot all about Mrs Dunstan.

'Let's go on the slide first,' he said.

It seemed a long way up the ladder, but at last Ben stood on the narrow platform at the top and looked down the shining slide to the ground far below. At that very moment Alfred popped his head out of the back of Ben's jacket and gave himself the most terrible fright.

'Eeeek!' he squeaked in horror. 'Where's the ground gone? Help!'

'Hang on to me tight,' shouted Ben, sitting on the slide and letting go of the sides. 'You're going to love this Alfred. *Wheeeee!*'

But Alfred didn't love it at all.

'I feel all funny and inside-out,' he complained to Ben. 'And I think I've left my tummy behind up there.'

'But that's the whole idea,' said, Ben in surprise. 'Never mind, we'll go on the roundabout instead. You'll like that, Alfred.'

But Alfred didn't like that either. It made him much too dizzy. 'I want to go on the swing,' he said. 'I want to go *now*!'

'All right,' sighed Ben. 'Sit on my cap. You'll be safe there.'

So Alfred crouched on the peak of the cap, gripping the edge tightly with his little front paws, as James started to push Ben on the swing.

'Higher,' yelled Ben. 'Higher!'

'Ooooooh,' groaned Alfred.

Ben felt as though he was flying through the sky as James pushed the swing strongly and sent him kicking high in the air. He could see right over the fence to his house and to his open bedroom window. 'I do hope Mrs Dustbin isn't looking for me,' he thought suddenly. 'What if she looks out of the window and sees me here?'

He pulled the peak of the cap down over his face as the swing slowed down, and Alfred tumbled off and landed with a thump on the soft grass.

'Umph!' he gasped. Then he picked himself up and blew the grass seeds off his whiskers.

'I'm going home,' he said. 'I've had enough.'

'Alfred!' Ben jumped off the swing. 'Come back!'

'Who's Alfred?' asked James.

'He's my mouse. He made me come here but now he doesn't want to go on anything.'

'I'm not surprised,' said James. 'Put him on the climbing-frame, that's the sort of thing a mouse likes.'

Ben scooped Alfred up gently and placed him on the frame.

'Now, that's more like it,' said Alfred. 'Why didn't you think of that before? This is going to be the best fun of all.'

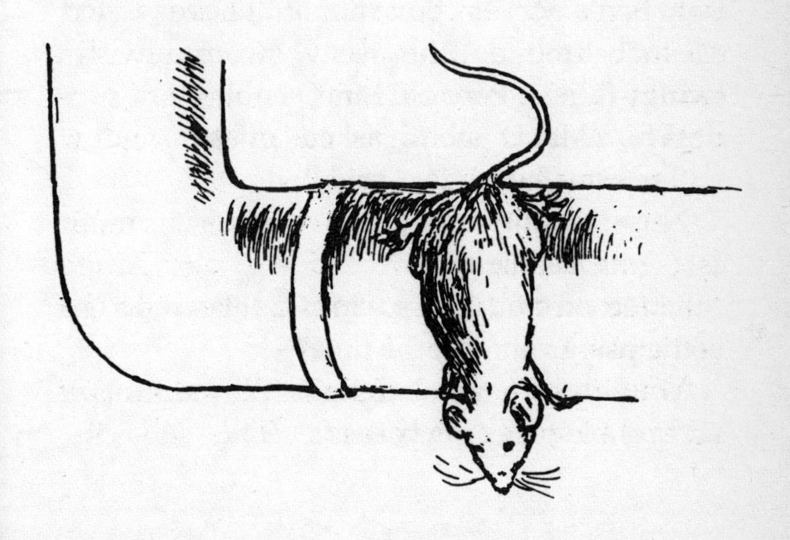

And it was. Ben couldn't believe it when the church clock struck twelve. 'How long have we been here?' he asked in alarm.

'Oh, about an hour,' said James. 'Want to go home?'

'Yes, please.' Ben stuffed Alfred in his pocket and ran out of the playground. Mrs Dustbin was bound to have noticed he was missing by now.

James took Ben's hand as they crossed the road. 'What's the big hurry?' he asked. 'Your mum won't be back yet.'

'I know, but . . .' Ben was too anxious to pretend any more. 'But Mrs Dustbin will be worrying.'

'She'll be worried sick,' said a gloomy voice from Ben's pocket. 'You shouldn't have wasted all that time on the nasty swoopy-swirly-swingy things. Poor old Mrs Dustbin.'

'Who's Mrs Dustbin?' asked James.

'She's my babysitter,' said Ben.

'No, she isn't,' said James. 'I am. Your mum asked me last night.'

Ben stood still. 'You mean I was allowed to go to the playground all the time?'

'Well, yes.' James laughed. 'Why not? You said you were feeling better.'

They were having second helpings of ice-cream when Mum came back. 'Had a good morning?' she asked.

'Great!' said Ben. 'Why didn't you tell me James was looking after me?'

'I tried to,' said Mum. 'I started to say, "Mrs Dunstan can't come, so James will be here instead," but you wouldn't listen, so I decided you could have a nice surprise.'

Ben licked his spoon thoughtfully. 'Good. James can look after me tomorrow.'

'No, he can't.' Mum smiled. 'I think you're quite well enough to go to school tomorrow.'

'I'll take you to the funfair on Saturday, if you like,' offered James as he went out the door. 'There's this massive fast roundabout with galloping horses.'

'Wow!' exclaimed Ben. 'We'd love that, wouldn't we, Alfred?'

Alfred closed his eyes and shuddered. 'I think I'll stay at home and look after your mum,' he said.

8 Alfred and the New Pet

On Saturday morning Alfred was not in a good mood.

'I suppose you're going to that dreadful noisy fair with that boy,' he said, 'and leaving me behind.'

'You didn't want to come,' said Ben. 'Sure you won't change your mind?'

'Quite sure,' said Alfred gloomily as the doorbell rang. 'I just hope you enjoy yourselves, that's all.'

'We will!' said Ben.

And they did. They screamed with fear on the ghost train and yelled with excitement on the bumper cars. They shouted with delight on the galloping horses and shrieked as they hung in the space ships.

And, finally, when they were both completely hoarse, Ben spent the last of his money on the darts.

Usually Ben wasn't very good at throwing.

But now, with James watching, and no Alfred to distract him, he hurled the darts straight at the board.

'How about that!' croaked James admiringly. 'Brilliant. You've won a goldfish.'

Ben carried the goldfish home proudly in its polythene bag. He raced into the kitchen. 'Mum, Mum, look what I've won!'

'Oh,' said Mum. She didn't sound quite as delighted as Ben had hoped. 'Well done. We'd better get the poor little fellow out of that bag and into something else.'

'I've got an old tank at home,' said James. 'I'll go and get it.'

Ben raced upstairs to show the fish to Alfred. But Alfred was not impressed. He sniffed suspiciously as Ben held out the bag.

'What is it?'

'It's a goldfish, of course. He's going to live in a tank in my room. Isn't he beautiful?'

'No,' said Alfred. 'He hasn't got ears and he hasn't got legs and he hasn't any fur at all. He definitely isn't beautiful. What does he do?'

'Well . . . he sort of swims up and down and . . . er . . . eats, and, well, . . . swims.'

'Huh.' Alfred sat back and examined the fish critically. 'Sounds pretty boring to me. What's he for?'

'For?' Ben thought about it. 'I don't know.'

'Exactly,' snapped Alfred. And he hopped behind his brick and pulled it to after him.

Ben trailed downstairs. 'I don't think Alfred likes my fish,' he said.

'Perhaps he's jealous,' said Mum. 'You'll have to make a fuss of him.'

That night Alfred didn't play in Ben's room. He didn't sleep in Ben's stripy sock either.

Ben lay in bed and thought about the gleaming little fish swimming up and down in the darkness. Alfred must have something wrong with his eyes if he couldn't see how beautiful he was.

Next morning Ben was woken by Alfred tickling his ear with his whiskers.

'That fish is still here,' said Alfred. 'Are you fed up with him yet?'

'Of course not,' said Ben. Then he added unwisely, 'I've always wanted a pet.'

Alfred nearly fell off the bed in disgust. 'A pet! What do you want a pet for when you've got a proper mouse like me for a friend? I suppose you'll want one of those stupid white mice in a cage next.'

Ben hesitated. 'But they're nice. And it could be a friend for you too, Alfred.'

'Never!' snorted Alfred.

The fish swam round his tank, ignoring all the fuss, his big eyes staring sideways through the glass. Alfred stared back.

'Call that a goldfish? He's not gold at all, he's all pale. I think you got a dud one there, Ben.'

'He's meant to be that colour,' said Ben. 'I'm calling him Sylvester Pearl, because he's all silvery and pearly.'

'Yuk!' replied Alfred.

Ben took great care of Sylvester Pearl. He fed him regularly and made sure that the tank was clean and had plenty of good, green weed, but Sylvester just did not seem to thrive. He swam slowly and unevenly through the fronds of weed and soon spent most of his day hiding behind a stone.

'I think he's lonely,' said Ben. 'Do you think we should get a friend for him, Mum?'

'Not yet,' said Mum. 'We want to make sure he's quite well. We wouldn't want his friend to catch anything.'

Then one morning Ben woke up to find Sylvester floating on his back on the surface of the water.

'Mum', he howled. 'Mum, come quick. I think something's wrong with Sylvester.'

Mum ran in and looked in the tank. Then she sat on the bed with Ben and put her arm round him.

'I'm afraid Sylvester is dead,' she said. 'I think he was quite an old fish. Too old to sit in a polythene bag in the heat of the fair. You rescued him and looked after him, but I think it was time for him to die peacefully.'

Ben stared miserably at the little fish. 'But I don't want him to be dead,' he wailed. 'Do something, Mum.'

'I wish I could.' Mum shook her head sadly. 'I can't make him better now, Ben.'

'We'll give him a proper funeral,' said Alfred, suddenly appearing on Ben's knee.

Ben wiped his nose on the back of his hand. 'We could bury him in the garden,' he agreed.

'Oh, no,' said Alfred. 'He's a fish, isn't he? We should bury him in a pond.'

Ben began to cheer up a little. 'Let's bury him in the river. He'd like that best of all. We could get there on the bus.'

'All right.' Mum picked Sylvester Pearl carefully out of the tank. 'You get dressed and I'll find a little box for him.'

'He can have my shoe box,' said Ben. 'I'll put stones in it to make it heavy.'

So Ben sat at the kitchen table and arranged the stones neatly on the bottom of the box. Then Mum laid Sylvester gently on top of the stones and Ben closed the lid of the box.

'Now', said Mum. 'We're not going out without breakfast. It will be ready in a minute.'

Alfred looked at the box on the table. 'I'd like a box like that. I could curl up in it and be cosy.'

'You could have Susie's box,' said Ben. 'She

left her new shoes here because it was raining and she didn't want to get them wet. I bet she'd let you have the box.'

'It's not as big as Sylvester's,' said Alfred.

'Yes, it is.' Ben put the boxes side by side. 'They're exactly the same.'

'Breakfast's ready,' said Mum. 'We'll have to be quick if we want to catch the bus.'

It was still and sunny by the river and there were lots of people fishing and walking their dogs. A big dog bounded up to them and snif-fed at the box.

'Bonzo! Come back here,' called the owner. He smiled at Ben. 'Don't worry, Bonzo is very friendly.'

Ben stroked the dog. 'I expect he can smell Sylvester.'

'Or me,' said a squeaky voice from Ben's pocket.

They walked round the bend in the river and stood on the edge of the bank. 'This would be a good place,' said Mum. 'Careful now.'

Ben stood for a moment and watched the river flow swiftly past. Then he lowered the box into the water.

'Goodbye, Sylvester Pearl,' he said. 'Rest in peace.'

The river caught the box and swirled it away and they watched it till it vanished from sight round the bend.

'It doesn't seem to be sinking,' said Alfred, peering out from Ben's pocket.

'It will.' Mum took Ben's hand. 'Let's walk

on a bit and feed the ducks. I've brought some bread.'

'I hope you brought some for me,' said Alfred. 'This river air does give you an appetite.'

Ben cried on the way home on the bus. 'I wish we'd had the funeral at home,' he wept. 'He's so far away now. I wish we'd buried him in the garden. I could have made him a gravestone.'

When they got back, Aunty Jo and Susie were waiting on the doorstep.

'We've come to pick up Susie's shoes,' said Aunty Jo. 'What's the matter with Ben?'

'Come in and have a cup of tea,' said Mum, 'and we'll tell you all about it.'

Aunty Joe and Susie were very sorry to hear about Sylvester. Talking to them made Ben feel better. But Alfred soon became impatient. 'What about my box?' he whispered. 'Ask if I can have it.'

Ben pushed the box across the table. 'Here are Susie's new shoes, Aunty Jo. But, could Alfred have the box?'

'Of course he can.' Aunty Jo lifted the lid. 'I'll take the shoes out. I'm longing to see them . . .!'

'What's wrong?' Mum leaned over her shoulder to look. 'Oh, no! Oh, Ben.'

'That's not my shoes,' said Susie. 'That's poor little Sylvester Pearl.'

Ben and Susie looked at each other.

'Well, if that's Sylvester Pearl . . .' said Susie.

'Mum,' said Ben, in a small voice. 'I think I may have buried Susie's shoes in the river by mistake.'

Susie's mouth opened into a large black square. 'Myyyyy SHOOOOOOES,' she roared.

'Stop that at once,' said Aunty Jo.

'We'll get you another pair, of course,' said Mum. 'Tomorrow.'

'We won't,' said Alfred. 'They were the last ones.'

But, luckily, Susie didn't hear.

Mum put the lid back on the box and sighed. 'We'll bury Sylvester in the garden after all,' she said.

Alfred was especially nice to Ben that night. He didn't zoom round on the cars as he usually did, but dragged the stripy sock on to Ben's pillow. 'I've come to cheer you up,' he said. 'That's what friends are for.'

They were almost asleep when Mum put her

head round the door. 'We've got visitors,' she said with a smile, and a big brown dog trotted eagerly into the room.

Ben sat up in bed. 'It's Bonzo! What's he doing here?'

'He's brought you these,' said his owner. And he held out a pair of shiny, black shoes. 'We saw the box floating by in the river so Bonzo jumped in and retrieved it. Your mother's name and address were on the bill inside one of the shoes.'

'They didn't even get wet,' said Ben happily. 'They're as good as new. Susie will be pleased. Clever, clever Bonzo.'

Later that night Alfred said, 'What's your mother done with that tank? Has she thrown it away?'

'No,' said Ben sleepily. 'She put it in the cupboard.'

'Perhaps she'll get you another fish one day. When you've got over Sylvester.'

'Don't want another fish,' muttered Ben. 'It won't be the same.'

'No, it won't be the same. But it will be all right, you'll see.'

Ben blinked at Alfred in surprise. 'I thought

you didn't like Sylvester?'

Alfred yawned casually. 'Oh, I got used to him, I suppose. And I'd rather have a fish than a dog any day.'

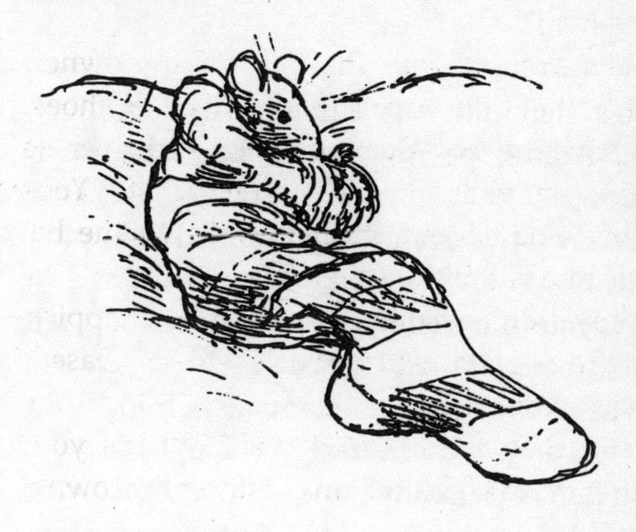

9 Alfred and Great-Aunt Lucy's Hat

'Who's that old lady kissing your mother?' asked Alfred, peering out of Ben's bedroom window.

'It's my Great-Aunt Lucy,' replied Ben, pulling at his coat. 'She's taking me and Susie to the cinema. I'd better go now, Alfred. I'll tell you all about it when I get back.'

'What about me?' demanded Alfred. 'You can't leave me out of a treat like that!'

But Ben had already gone without him.

Alfred darted out of the window and skidded down the drainpipe as Ben ran along the front path.

'Wait for me, Ben' he called. 'I'm coming too. I've never been to a film.'

'You can't.' Ben looked back at his great-aunt. 'She's scared of mice. Go home, Alfred.'

Alfred jumped into Ben's coat pocket. 'I'm coming too,' he repeated stubbornly.

Ben sighed. 'All right. But you have got to

behave yourself.'

'I will,' promised Alfred. 'I'll be so good you won't even know I'm there.'

And Alfred was good. At first.

He was very good on the bus. He stayed quietly in Ben's pocket and didn't even peep out once during the whole journey. But, then, the bus was very crowded and Alfred never did like crowds. Susie had to sit on Great-Aunt Lucy's lap and Ben stood, squashed against them, hanging on to the back of their seat with his nose bumping into the bunch of artificial cherries on Great-Aunt Lucy's hat. Ben loved cherries and these ones looked ripe and juicy and very real. It made him hungry to look at them.

'It's lucky Alfred can't see those. He'd try to eat them,' thought Ben. 'I wonder what they taste like . . .?' and he gave them a gentle lick as the bus swung him forward.

Alfred was still being good when they got off the bus and, apart from some small muffled cries of 'Are we nearly there?', there was hardly a squeak out of him all the way to the cinema.

Outside the cinema there was a long queue. 'Oh dear!' said Great-Aunt Lucy. 'What a nuisance.'

The children didn't mind. Queuing was part of the fun. But Alfred was not a patient mouse. He stuck his head out of Ben's pocket and looked round excitedly. 'Pssst! What's going on? Why have we stopped?'

Great-Aunt Lucy smiled at the children. 'Not long now, dears. Look, the queue is moving. We'll be inside very soon.'

'Get down, Alfred,' muttered Ben furiously. 'You promised, remember . . .?'

'All right, all right.' Alfred waved a paw and vanished back into the pocket. 'Don't fuss! I'll stay put.'

But he didn't.

It would take a stronger mouse than Alfred to

stay in a dark pocket, on his very first visit to the cinema, without wanting to have a look at what was going on. It was bad enough listening to the crackling of sweet packets, though Ben did remember to pass him down a big puffy bit of popcorn, but when the film began and he could hear the most tantalizing and mysterious sounds of voices and music, Alfred could bear it no longer. He crept up Ben's coat and sat on his knee. All he could see from there was the seat in front, so he ran up to Ben's shoulder. It was still no good.

'I can't see,' he complained in a loud, hoarse whisper. 'That lady in front of us should brush her hair flat.'

The lady turned round and glared at Ben. 'Shhh!' she said.

'Be quiet, Alfred!' Ben shrank back in embarrassment and moved the mouse to his other shoulder. 'Try that.'

'That's worse,' said Alfred, in an even louder whisper. 'That man has such big ears that I can't see past them.'

'I told you not to come,' said Ben unsympathetically. 'Get back in my pocket and go to sleep.'

Alfred didn't bother to answer. Sleep indeed!

When he could be watching his very first film. He climbed on to the back of the next seat and then ran up Great-Aunt Lucy's back and sat down comfortably on her hat. That was much better. He could see beautifully and there was even a bunch of cherries there for him to nibble. He picked one and chewed it, but it tasted horrible, so he spat out the bits.

'Alfred,' hissed Ben. 'Come back at *once*!'

'Everything all right, dear?' Great-Aunt Lucy leaned over Ben and patted his hand. Ben longed to snatch Alfred off her hat but he didn't dare.

The film was very exciting. It was so exciting that Ben forgot all about Alfred and Alfred completely forgot about the time.

When the film ended it was too late to get back to Ben in the general rush for the exits, so Alfred stayed where he was and was carried along on the hat through the door and out into the street. Ben got quite a shock when he glanced up at Great-Aunt Lucy and suddenly saw Alfred gazing out happily over the brim of her hat.

'That bad mouse!' thought Ben. 'Why can't he do as he's told? I do hope he keeps still. It would be awful if anyone noticed a mouse running about on Great-Aunt Lucy's best hat.'

At that moment two girls walked past. 'Look at that!' said one. 'Looks so real, doesn't it. I've never seen a hat like that before.'

Alfred stared glassily in front of him and didn't move a whisker as Great-Aunt Lucy smiled proudly. Those cherries did look real, she thought, and it certainly was an unusual hat.

Ben's mother and Aunty Jo were waiting outside the cinema and the children rushed up to them excitedly. If Ben had looked he might have seen Alfred clinging desperately to the cherries, as Great-Aunt Lucy bobbed about being hugged and kissed and thanked. And if he had listened he might have heard Alfred calling to him. But Ben was hopping up and down chattering busily. He wasn't thinking about Alfred at all.

That evening, Ben was going up to bed when his mother said, 'You'll have to tell Alfred all about the film tonight.'

'Alfred!' Ben stopped dead. 'Alfred knows all about it. He saw it too. He came in my pocket.'

'Oh, that naughty mouse!' Mum exclaimed in annoyance. 'Where is he now?'

'I think he's on Great-Aunt Lucy's hat,' said Ben. 'That's where he was in the cinema. Poor Alfred, he must be starving. I do hope he hasn't eaten all those nasty cherries.'

'So do I,' said Mum. 'Get your coat, Ben.

We'll go and see Great-Aunt Lucy right away. We'll pick some flowers for her to say "thank you".'

Great-Aunt Lucy was very surprised to see them again so soon, and delighted with the flowers. 'How lovely,' she said, 'I was just having a nice cup of tea in the kitchen. Come and join me.'

'Where's your hat?' asked Ben.

Great-Aunt Lucy beamed at him. 'On my bed,' she said. 'Do you want to look at it again? Really, that hat was such a success today! Everyone was pointing it out. And the funniest thing happened . . . when I took it off I saw some of the cherries had been eaten. A bird must have thought they were real and pecked them as I walked along and I never even noticed. Bring my hat in here, Ben, and show Mummy.'

Ben ran to the bedroom and picked up the hat. There was no sign of Alfred.

'Alfred,' he whispered. 'Are you there?'

A quivering pink nose and two beady black eyes appeared from under the remains of the bunch of cherries.

'I thought you were never coming,' said

Alfred accusingly. 'Fancy forgetting me like that. I hope you've brought me something to eat. I've had nothing but these disgusting cherries since lunch-time. I'm sure there's something wrong with them.'

'Oh, dear,' said Ben.

'Don't worry,' said Alfred. 'I've been very sick, so I should be all right now.'

Ben's mother admired the hat and put it quickly in a plastic carrier bag. 'I'll sew another bunch of cherries on it for you,' she told Great-Aunt Lucy. 'It will look as good as new.'

It was dark as they walked home and Ben was tired.

'You tell young Alfred to do as he's told in future,' said Mrs Hope.

'I have told him,' said Ben, 'and he says he's learnt his lesson.'

Ben's mother laughed and looked at Alfred as he rode along tucked cosily into the collar of Ben's jersey.

'That'll be the day!' she said.

10 Alfred Goes to the Party

'It's Susie's birthday today,' said Ben. 'She's having a party. We're all going out for hamburgers.'

'Ohhh!' Alfred sat up and twitched his whiskers. 'Yum, yum. I love hamburgers. I'll eat all round the outside of yours and you can have the middle.'

'No,' said Ben.

'No one will see me,' said Alfred. 'You can hold the hamburger in front of your pocket, and I'll pop my head out now and again and take a bite.'

'You're not coming,' said Ben firmly. 'Not after the way you behaved at the cinema. Mum says you've got to stay at home in future.'

'That wasn't my fault.' Alfred turned his back and sulked. 'I think you're mean. You never take me anywhere now.'

'Come and see Susie's cake,' said Ben. 'Mum has just finished icing it.' And he picked Alfred up and carried him into the kitchen.

'Huh!' muttered Alfred. 'Boring, boring, boring. Who wants to see a stupid old cake.'

'You do,' said Ben. 'Look.'

'That's not a cake,' gasped Alfred. 'That's a house. A real little chocolate house just the right size for me.'

'It's a cake all right,' said Ben proudly. 'Mum's good at icing things.'

They gazed at it longingly.

'Liquorice drainpipes,' sighed Alfred. 'And look at all those sugar flowers. Shall we pick one or two to make it look more natural?'

'No,' said Ben.

'You don't think it would be better with just one chimney?' Alfred suggested hopefully, licking his lips.

'N–no.'

A moment later Alfred said, 'No one would miss that little window at the side.' He tapped it gently with his small, pink paw. 'Oh, dear. It's fallen off. I'd better eat it before your mum sees.'

'Sees what?' asked Mum as she came into the kitchen. 'Quick, Ben, I can hear Susie at the front door. Leave the cake on its tray and cover it up with this box. Don't forget to put Alfred back in your room, she added.

'He's gone,' said Ben. 'I think he's sulking because he can't come too.'

'Poor Alfred, we'll save him a bit of cake. Now, run and open the door. We don't want to miss our lift to the party.'

The hamburger restaurant was bright and new, and crowded with people.

Ben's mother put the tray on the seat next to her.

'What's in that box?' asked Susie.

'Wait and see,' said Aunty Jo. 'You can open it after you have all had your hamburgers.'

Susie had invited six children to her party. They were dressed in their best clothes and were on their best behaviour. They put on their party hats and ate their meal quietly. Ben blew bubbles into his milk shake through his straw. He felt sorry for Susie. It was not a very lively party.

'Now for that box,' said Susie.

'Close your eyes for one minute everybody.' Aunty Joe cleared a space on the table as Mum searched in her bag for the candles.

All the children sat obediently with their eyes tightly shut – all except Susie and Ben, who watched impatiently as Aunty Jo lifted the box off the cake.

'Aaaah, isn't it lovely,' sighed Susie in delight. 'Oh, thank you, it's what I've always wanted. A dear little mouse house.'

'A dear little what?' Ben's mother looked up from her bag.

Ben stared at the cake with an awful sinking feeling in his tummy. One of the beautiful high chimneys had gone and so had the shiny liquorice drainpipe, and a whole layer of tiles from the roof had been neatly nibbled away. Where the front door had been was a crumbly hole and inside it, fast asleep, was a very small, very fat mouse.

'Alfred!' shouted Ben. 'You bad, bad mouse. You've eaten Susie's cake.'

At once the other children opened their eyes.

'A mouse?' exclaimed Tom. 'Show us, quick.'

'Where is he?' asked Kim. 'I can't see a mouse.'

Susie pointed at the cake. 'He's there,' she said. 'Look!'

But Alfred had gone.

Ben scanned the restaurant desperately. If only there weren't so many people. Alfred could be anywhere. Ben imagined Alfred twisting and swerving among the shiny tables, dazzled by the bright lights, deafened by the noise, and terrified by all the big, heavy feet that could step on him so easily. 'Help, help!' he wailed. 'Oh, Mum, my Alfred is lost.'

'No, he isn't,' said Mum. 'Alfred will turn up. He always does.'

'Who's Alfred?' asked a fat lady in a fur coat

at the next table.

'My mouse,' said Ben. 'He's run away. He must be here somewhere but we don't know where.'

The lady looked most upset. She lifted her feet off the ground and peered anxiously down at the floor.

'Come on, everyone!' called Susie. 'We've got to find Ben's mouse.'

'There he is!' shouted Tom. 'On the counter . . . now he's gone behind the till.'

'No!' yelled Kim. 'He's running along the back of that chair . . . Oh! He's fallen off. I think he's in that shopping basket.'

'No, he isn't. He's on the litter bin,' said Ezra. 'Well, he was a minute ago.'

The children jumped down eagerly from their chairs and spread out through the restaurant. Soon, one by one, all the other children there joined them in the search. They crawled along the seats and under the tables, and in and out of the grown-ups' legs. Their paper hats fell off, and they got hot and dusty and untidy. They bumped their heads and fell over each other. They had a perfectly wonderful time but they didn't find Alfred.

Suddenly Susie stood on a chair and pointed at the fat lady in the fur coat, who was just about to take a big bite of her burger. 'That lady,' announced Susie in a very loud voice, 'has got Alfred in her bun. I can see his tail hanging out.'

The fat lady dropped her bun with a scream and Ben snatched it up at once. He raised the top and peered inside. There, sure enough,

was Alfred, looking very pleased with himself, lying back on the remains of some lettuce, and licking melted cheese off his paws.

'Now *that's* what I call a cheeseburger,' said Alfred contentedly. 'Pop me in your pocket before those children see me, Ben. I've had quite enough adventures for today.'

Alfred yawned and hiccupped all the way home. 'I'm worn out,' he groaned, 'and I've got a dreadful tummy-hic-ache.'

'Serves you right for being so greedy.' Ben

was not sympathetic. 'You spoiled Susie's cake and you ruined her party.'

'No, I didn't,' said Alfred indignantly. 'Susie loved her mouse house and all the children said it was the most hic-citing party they had ever been to. I was a great suc-hic-cess.'

'Well, from now on you stay at home when I go out,' said Ben. 'I'm not taking you anywhere ever again. Do you hear me, Alfred?'

But Alfred was fast asleep.